This igloo belongs to:

Published in 2019
by Igloo Books Ltd
Cottage Farm
Sywell
NN6 0BJ
www.igloobooks.com

GOL002 0319
2 4 6 8 10 9 7 5 3 1
ISBN 978-1-78905-666-2

Written by Melanie Joyce
Illustrated by Gabi Murphy

Cover designed by Lee Italiano
Interiors designed by Stephanie Drake
Edited by Will Putnam

Printed and manufactured in China

Tickle Me

igloobooks

Tickle me because
I love it.

Tickle me because
it's fun.

Tickle me and tell me . . .

. . . I'm your special little one.

Tickle me and chase me under the mango trees.

One . . .

two . . .

three . . .

four . . .

. . . tickle me, please!

Tickle me on a Tuesday.

Tickle me every day.

Tickle me
when I sleep.

Tickle me
when we play.

Tickle me outside.

Tickle me at home.

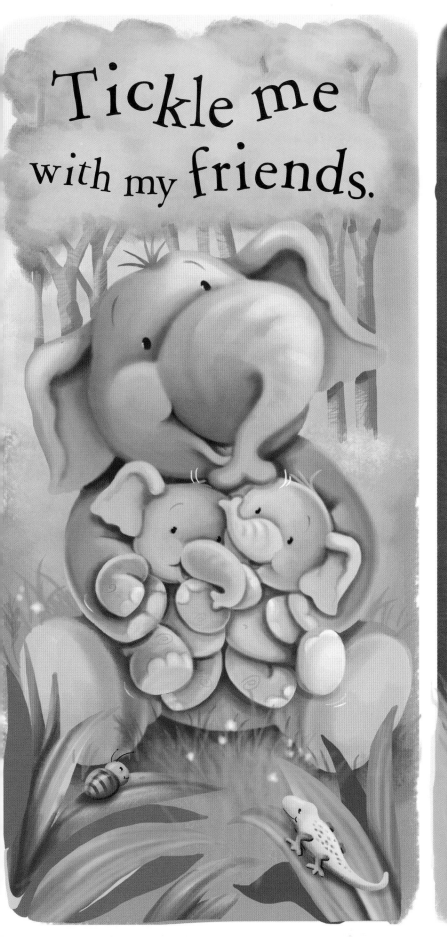

Tickle me
with my friends.

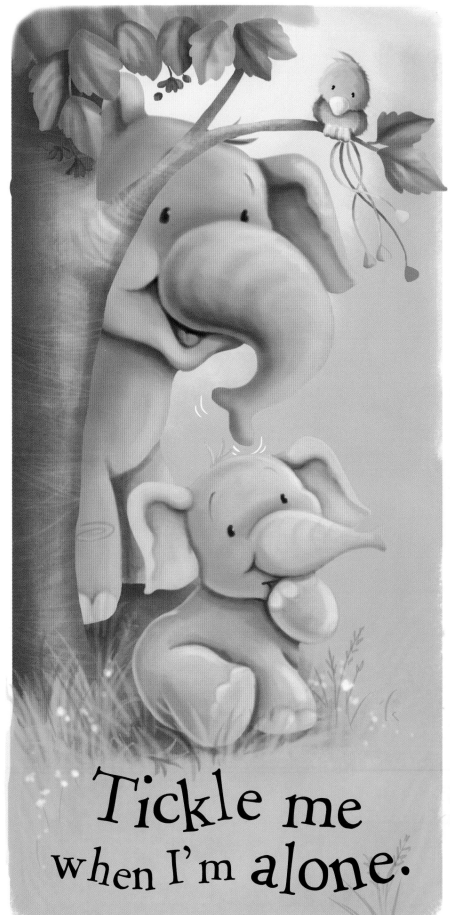

Tickle me
when I'm alone.

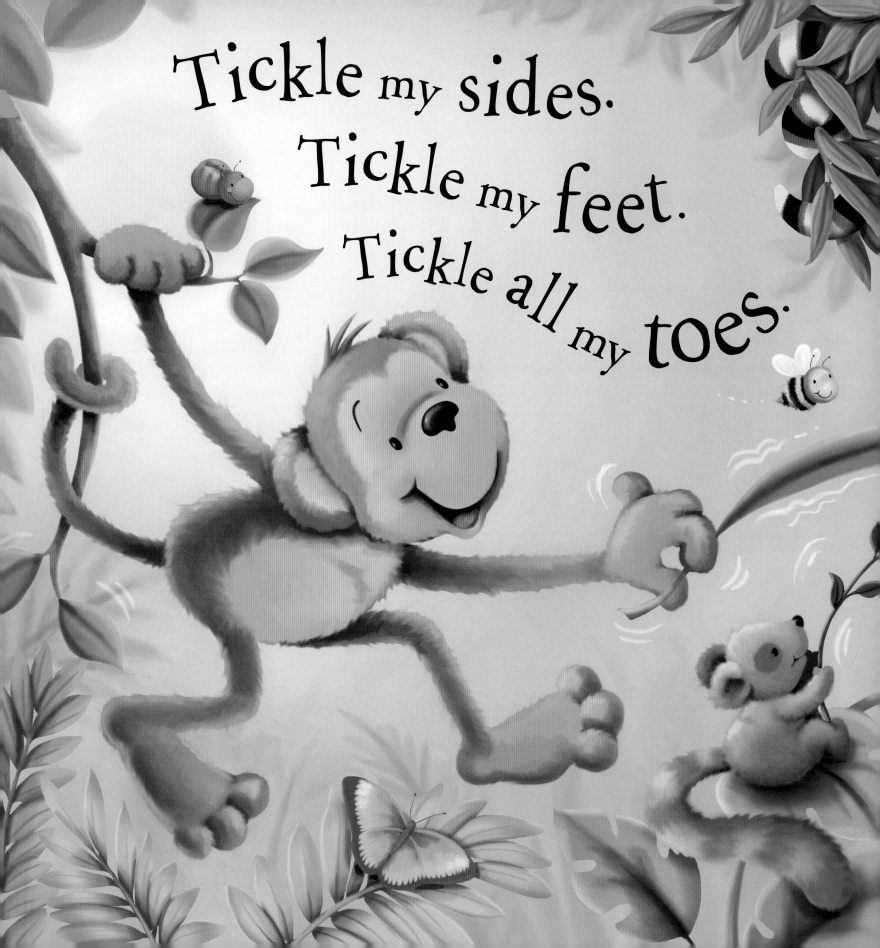

Tickle my sides.
Tickle my feet.
Tickle all my toes.

Tickle me all the way up to my wiggly nose.

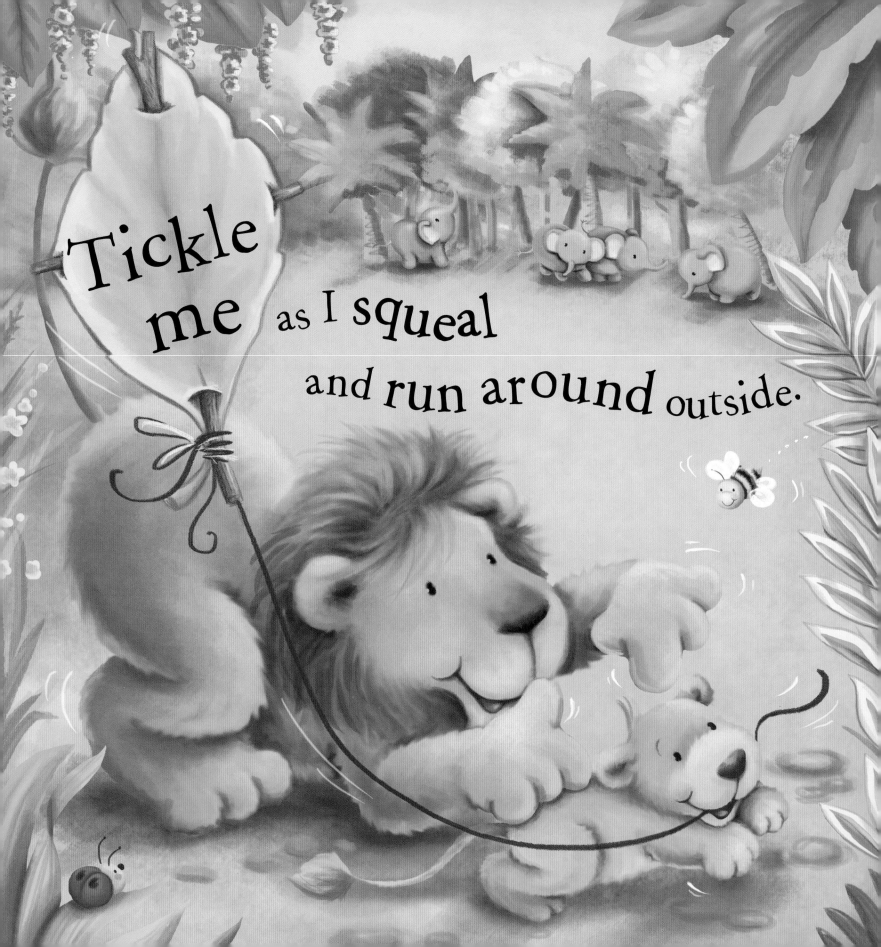

Tickle me as I squeal and run around outside.

Tickle me as I count to ten and peek as you run to hide.

Tickle me when I find you . . .

. . . so we roll around and giggle.

Tickle me until I curl up in a ball . . .

. . . and wriggle.

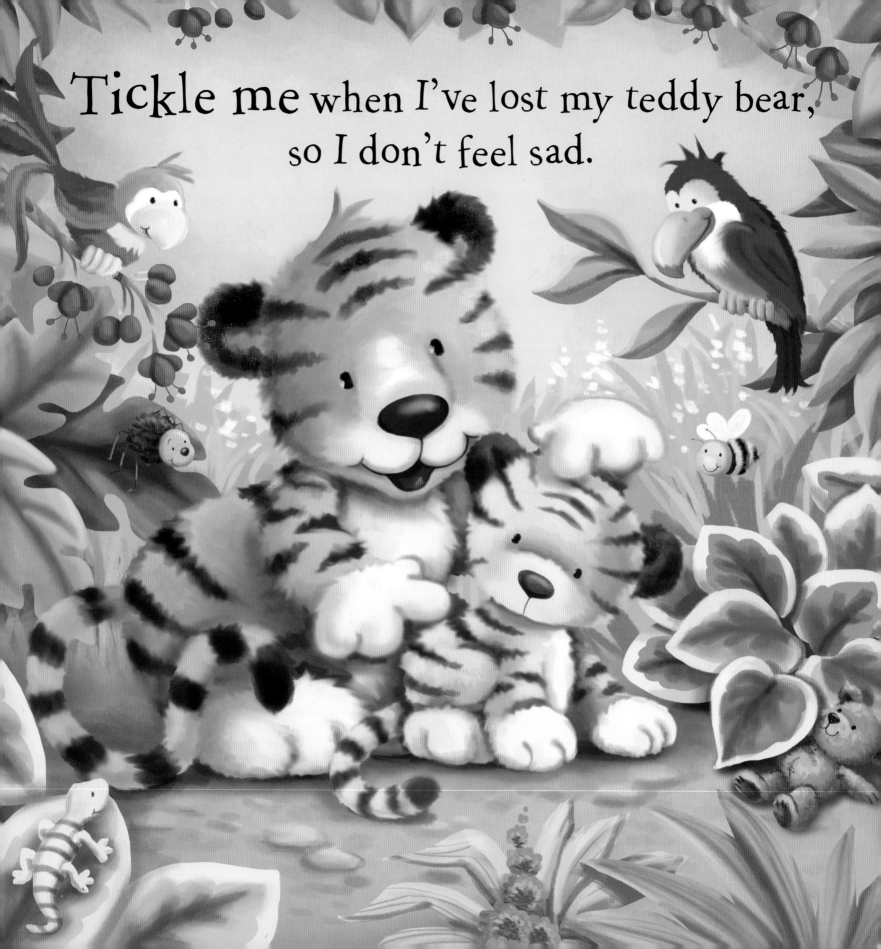

Tickle me when I've lost my teddy bear, so I don't feel sad.

Tickle me and tell me . . .

It's really not
so **bad.**

Tickle me in the evening and say . . .

"Come on, time for bed."

Tickle me when I say,
"No, I want to play instead!"

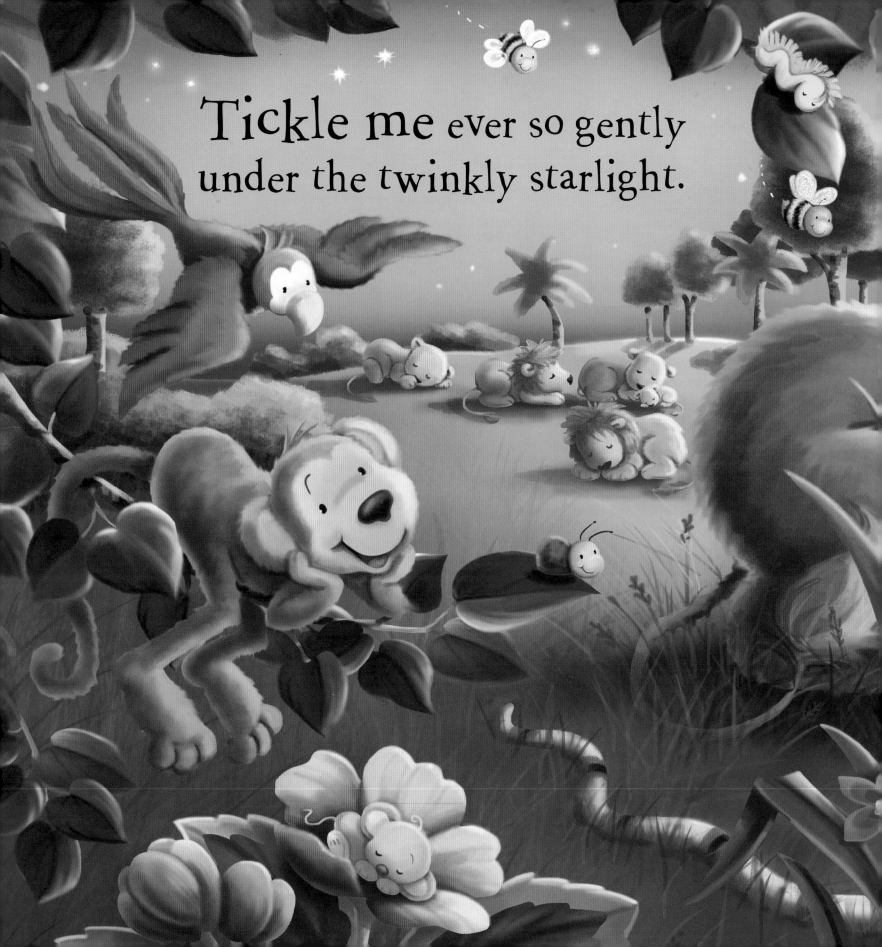

Tickle me ever so gently
under the twinkly starlight.

Tickle me very softly, kiss me, and say . . .

"Good night."

Sleep tight.